About th ‖‖‖‖‖‖‖‖‖‖‖‖‖‖‖‖‖
D0461808

Mahul is an expert on luxury and has edited the column, for a leading newspaper, along with writing on luxury in leading newspapers and magazines. His debut on luxury – *Decoding Luxe* – has received praises from eminent authors, editors and industrialists, along with stalwarts such as Amitabh Bachchan, Ratan Tata, Bibek Debroy, Hon Governor of West Bengal Shri Keshari Nath Tripathi and Hon Chief Minister of West Bengal, Ms Mamata Banerjee.

Mahul's directorial debut *Post It!* has been selected at various international film festivals. As an actor, his debut film was screened at 69th Cannes Film Festival in 2016. His debut Bengali feature film *Hoytoh Manush Noi* was released in 2018.

He heads CSR, branding and corporate communications for a Tata Steel and SAIL venture – mjunction. He is a member of Confederation of Indian Industry – CII Young Indians.

Mahul has been a Senior Editor with leading media houses such as India partner of New York Times, Economic Times, Reuters and CNBC TV18.

Mahul has won the prestigious 'Brand Leadership Award' and 'Ecommerce Communication Leader of the Year' Award in 2017 and 'Young Achiever Award' in the National Awards for Excellence in Corporate Communication in 2016.

Hailing from a Brahmo family in Kolkata, Mahul was a student of St Xavier's College, Calcutta, with a Masters in International Economics from University of Calcutta and a PhD in Economics. He is an alumnus of MICA and University of Cambridge Judge Business School Executive Education. He is an avid golfer.

🐦: @mahulbrahma

✉: mahul.brahma@gmail.com

f: /AuthorMahul/

Praise for the author and his work

Wishing Mahul continued success in all that he endeavors.

—Amitabh Bachchan

Let more writings come through the pen of Mahul.

—Shri Keshari Nath Tripathi,
Hon. Governor of West Bengal

You and your writings always have all my blessings Mahul.

—Smt Mamata Banerjee,
Hon Chief Minister of West Bengal

I wish Mahul's book all the success.

—Ratan N. Tata

Congratulations and best wishes to you for your new book Dark Luxe. I am sure it will be a great success!

—Harish Bhat,
Author, Brand Custodian of Tata Sons

Mahul Brahma's sequel Dark Luxe is a bigger eye opener as he now goes backstage and presents the dark costs paid by many of those who aspire to succeed in the bewitching business of luxury and glamour. He speaks with characteristic candour and does not moralise, but hides nothing. A must read.

– Jawhar Sircar, Former CEO, Prasar Bharati

With Dark Luxe, Mahul has ventured into an area which remains well guarded and never talked about. The stories are a refreshing as well as spine-chilling work of fiction. Blood and luxe is indeed a heady concoction. I wish it all the success.

– Nirvik Singh, Chairman & CEO,
Asia Pacific, Middle East & Africa, GREY Group

Decoding Luxe is very different from existing literature on luxury, which consists primarily of catalogues. The author has a lucid and jargon-free style of explaining strategic moves in the luxury market, with a dash of humour. The book is a must-read for luxury retailers and students who want to understand the Indian market and consumers better.

—Surya Sarathi Ray, *Financial Express*

There isn't much written about luxury brands and luxury buying in India. And that's the gap that author Mahul Brahma fills with his book, Decoding Luxe. *In the book he takes the reader through a plethora of things associated with luxury brands. The writer brings out interesting and lesser-known facts about luxury shopping and does a good job of it. It's a must read for those who want to know anything about luxury.*

—Himika Chaudhuri, *HT City Delhi*

The romance of luxury has waited long for such a deft rendition of insight and eloquence.

—Kunal Basu, Author

iii

For me, Mahul's book Decoding Luxe *works as a much-needed cultural history of dazzle. The book is an essential step in understanding the tug and pull of a class-based society, a brilliant attempt at unveiling its various mysteries. The book could become one of the most important devices to understand the codes and the unseen forces that drive our society. A quiet voice that will have a thundering impact. An essential read.*

—Sarnath Banerjee, Graphic Novelist, Author

My friend Mahul's attempt to understand the dynamics of this market seems timely. I was pleasantly surprised to find that Mahul has worked hard to decode even the customer. In a market that is ready to explode, understanding the customer could well be the key to retaining her, and to expanding the scope of the luxury segment itself.

—Sachin Kalbag, Editor, *The Hindu* (Mumbai)

Mahul's book is a seminal and in depth work that feels the pulse, not just of the luxury industry but also that of the consumer. He does a huge favour to both – makes life easier for the brands by telling them how to tap into the Indian psyche further on one hand and whets the appetite of buyers excited by luxury on the other. Mahul's style is lucid, his analysis impeccable. This book is a must have.

—Kounteya Sinha, Former United Kingdom
Correspondent, *Times of India*

Mahul has crafted a lovely story around luxury in India from the Maharajas to the newer rich. This is a great read for anyone interested in the science of vanity and what makes luxury tick. All luxury brands want to be aspirational without alienating people or being aloof. This book has many illustrative examples to satiate your curiosity.

—D. Shivakumar, Former Chairman
and CEO, PepsiCo India

Mahul has a great love for luxury watches and had almost twisted my wrist a couple of times to check out my watch. He has a very lucid style of writing. Decoding Luxe is a fantastic read and it gives a fresh perspective to luxe. He has been able to address some of the core issues that any luxury retailer needs to know to do business in this country. I believe this will be a good manual for luxury retailers and will be able to create tangible value for them.

—Sanjiv Goenka, Past President CII & Chairman,
RP-SG Group

Mahul is a gifted writer. He is very passionate about luxury. I loved the way he has been able draw a parallel between the life cycle of a luxury brand and Shakespeare's description of The Seven Ages of Man. The book gives a very unique perspective to luxury. Decoding Luxe is a great read and I am certain it will be a success.

—Harshavardhan Neotia, Past President, FICCI &
Chairman, Ambuja Neotia Group

Mahul has been a prolific writer since his journalism days. I liked the way he has been able to introduce some unconventional ideas and thoughts such as e-commerce will not succeed as far as luxury retailing is concerned despite it being a successful retailing model in the country. I am certain Decoding Luxe *will be greatly appreciated.*

—Hemant Kanoria, CMD,
SREI Infrastructure Finance Ltd

I love the way Mahul deconstructs the mystical world of luxury with his simple, direct, matter-of-fact lucid style of narration. Mahul has chosen an area where there is very limited literature globally and has taken a holistic view of luxe. Something that was much-needed. Decoding Luxe *is a very well written book and I am sure it will be a great success.*

—Arnab Chakraborty, National Director,
UN-EmpretecProgramme for India

Dark Luxe

Mahul Brahma

Srishti
PUBLISHERS & DISTRIBUTORS

SRISHTI PUBLISHERS & DISTRIBUTORS
Registered Office: N-16, C.R. Park
New Delhi – 110 019
Corporate Office: 212A, Peacock Lane
Shahpur Jat, New Delhi – 110 049
editorial@srishtipublishers.com

First published by
Srishti Publishers & Distributors in 2018

Printed and bound in India

Contents

Foreword
by Dr Bibek Debroy

*D*eep *into that darkness peering, long I stood there wondering, fearing, doubting, dreaming dreams no mortal ever dared to dream before.*

In the Prologue, Mahul Brahma quotes from Edgar Allen Poe's 'The Raven'. I found the choice of the poem most appropriate. The first lines are,

> *Once upon a midnight dreary, while I pondered, weak and weary,*
>
> *Over many a quaint and curious volume of forgotten lore...*
> and later,
>
> *Ah, distinctly I remember it was in the bleak December...*

It was indeed in bleak December that I read the first draft of this curious volume about deluxe-related lore and gore. If there is one person who is eminently qualified to write about deluxe and luxury products, it is Mahul. He has been writing and commenting on them for years, and he has already authored a delightful non-fiction book titled *Decoding Luxe*.

But this is fiction. At least one story is inspired by a real life incident – the one of the Maharaja of Alwar (Jai Singh) and six Rolls Royce cars used to cart garbage. That incident has a happy ending. Rolls Royce was so concerned at the company's image suffering that it gave the Maharaja six other cars free of cost, so that the luxury cars would no longer be used for garbage disposal. I presume the other stories may also have their roots in real life incidents, but none that I could immediately identify. However, there are no happy endings. For the purposes of this collection, the author has gone over to the dark side. The stories are told from the perspective of luxury products. It is by no means easy to define a luxury product. Stated simply, if it is available to everyone, it is not a luxury product. Rarefied possession is the key. The set of luxury products that figure in this collection are a princess cut diamond from Tiffany's, an Empress yacht (it is now called Indian Empress), 1952 Dom Perignon Champagne, a Louis Vuitton trunk, an unidentified logo, Hummer H3 (this has shades of the Maharaja of Alwar story too), a fake Rolex, a deer-skin wallet from Venice, a Rolls Royce Phantom, a Writers Edition Montblanc pen and a pair of golden scissors made by a master goldsmith. Often, luxury products are equated with brands and these are global. Accordingly, Mahul's stories are often set abroad; some in a few rare instances, in India. When I think of various kinds of luxury products, I wonder if there might have been a story with a perfume or fragrance too. The rest of the spectrum is covered, with counterfeit products also thrown in.

What do the rich and the famous do? Pretty much what everyone else does – 'Birth, and copulation, and death. That's all, that's all, that's all, that's all, birth, and copulation, and death.' And these incidents (including birth) are described from the perspectives of these luxury products, with both copulation and death, more often than not, forcibly inflicted. That's the dark side at work. Read continuously at one stretch, it may seem a trifle gruesome and grisly, like watching several Ingmar Bergman films one after another. However, these are independent stories and needn't be read that way. That will help transcend the macabre.

As an aside, there are several remarkable coincidences between James Bond films and the Beatles. For instance, both records and films were born on 5 October 1962. I mention this because the author quotes Sean Connery from Goldfinger: "My dear girl, there are some things that just aren't done; such as drinking Dom Perignon'53 above the temperature of 38 degrees Fahrenheit. That's as bad as listening to the Beatles without earmuffs."

But this is good reading, irrespective of whether you can afford to drink Dom Perignon.

Dr Bibek Debroy
Author, Economist,
Chairman-Prime Minister's
Economic Advisory Council

Foreword
by Himika Chaudhuri

Mahul's first book *Decoding Luxe* was a delight for people like us, who have been reporting on and working around luxury brands for years. The book opened up really interesting aspects of the business of luxury and gave a well-researched view of what goes into the making of a niche brand, how it curates its image, anoints new consumers into the brand's fold, reinvents itself with time. It also had interesting anecdotes of indulgences by Indian royals and the neo-rich. Indeed, the book is a crisp, clear and well-researched commentary of luxury brands in India. The only mention of the dark side of luxury was perhaps his chapter on how fake luxe products have flooded the market and how to identify them.

However, with his new book, *Dark Luxe*, Mahul transcends boundaries and steps into the genre of fiction writing and chooses to tell gory tales from the lives of those who live in the lap luxury. *Dark Luxe*, as he has aptly named it, holds a sense of intrigue in the title and the stories live up to it beautifully. Interestingly, Mahul uses the pieces of luxury, among many things, a Tiffany ring, a luxury yacht, and a bottle of Dom Perignon 52 as storytellers. It is these precious pieces that open up and share the dark stories in the lives of their masters – stories of sex, murder, betrayal and more. So, whether it is an LV trunk of a Nawab that bears the body of his girlfriend who he rapes and then murders or a Tiffany's engagement ring that reveals the story of a jealous woman who gets her friend killed so as to marry her fiancé, the sense of mystery and intrigue is intact in every short story. For the erratic, busy reader, the advantage is that one can start, stop and pick up the tome again, without there being a sense of a break.

Each story has a classic twist and an interesting storyline. When I began to read the chapters, so as to be able to write this foreword, I found myself gliding from chapter to chapter, unable to stop.

Himika Chaudhuri
Editor, Commercial Content
Hindustan Times

Foreword
by Kounteya Sinha

His first book talked about an obsession.
His second will tell you how far a person is willing to go to feed that obsession.

Social anthropologist and one of modern day's most astute consumer behavioral experts – Mahul Brahma dazzled us with his first book *Decoding Luxe* – a seminal work that revealed the obsession India had with luxury brands.

It was one of those books that leave you craving for more – a heady cocktail, I must say.

It could have a somewhat psychedelic effect on your mind – the inability of being able to afford a Louis Vuitton or a Gucci till then, could give sudden way to an overwhelming desire in you to push all your financial limits to actually own one.

Brahma is now back with a sequel to that bestseller and calls it *Dark Luxe*.

Having travelled most parts of the world spread over six continents as a journalist and a photographer for nearly two decades, experiencing luxury at the highest of levels in the farthest of places, I couldn't agree more to the insight delivered by the master storyteller in Brahma. I remember hearing a friend who worked in a flagship store in Delhi of one of the world's most iconic fashion labels telling me how the rich would walk into a store and brashly shout out, "Give me everything in every size you have". He or she didn't really care about what they were buying. They just knew they had hordes of money to get rid of before the sun rose again the next morning. And what better way than to splurge on buying an entire store of a high value fashion label – enough fodder to last one whole evening of social folk lore.

I was based in Britain as Times of India's London correspondent for over three years and saw how rich Indians overtook the Russians to become the richest landlords in Britain's most expensive commercial district – Mayfair. Indian purchasers became the largest group of overseas buyers with Indian billionaires having invested 881 million pounds in central London properties in just 18 months till the end of 2016.

This obsession with luxury is only expected to grow with latest economic forecasts predicting that in another 10 years-time, India will overtake wealth havens like United Kingdom and Germany to become the fourth richest country in the world. India is expected to record a massive 200% increase in wealth growth over the next 10 years – higher than any other country in the world. India recorded the highest percentage growth in wealth creation in a single year – between 2016 and 2017 – at 25%. This now makes India the sixth richest country in the world, below UK and Germany, who are placed at fourth and fifth, respectively.

India's total wealth is at present $8230 billion and is expected to rise to $24,691 billion by 2027, overtaking UK which will have $10,911 billion (fifth richest) and Germany $10,626 billion (sixth richest).

In another seven years, India is expected to have six global megacities and 41 major cities all connected through high speed corridors which will provide seamless transportation of luxury goods and services. This is bound to spur an obscene amount of spending in the luxury goods market.

The interesting point to note then would be to see at what levels Indian consumers are willing to go or stoop to be the proud owners of that limited edition clutch bag or a sports car.

That only time can tell.

But if you're not willing to wait that long, I suggest you pick up Brahma's latest book to maybe get an early edition peek into the future.

This could surely save you an all-nighter at a never ending serpentine queue outside Macy's or an Apple store during the next Black Friday sale.

Kounteya Sinha
Photographer,
Former UK and Europe Correspondent – *The Times of India*
Contributing Editor – *The National Geographic*

Foreword
by Prof Aloke Kumar

"There was no pleasure like being envied on a mass scale."

—Anna Godbersen, The Luxe

L ike alter-ego in literature, the book *Dark Luxe* is the alter-book to *Decoding Luxe*.

Mahul Brahma has penned a fascinating book relating to the ugliness of luxe. In the mold of his acclaimed *Decoding Luxe*, renowned luxe critic explores the monstrous side through fictional short stories.

What is the voyeuristic impulse behind our attraction to the gruesome and the horrible? Where does the magnetic appeal of the sordid and the scandalous come from? Brahma's captivating storytelling skills combine in this ingenious study of the *Dark Luxe*, revealing that what we're most attracted to subliminally is what we often shield ourselves from and crave in everyday life is also the most horrifying.

Guy de Maupassant, the French Writer, is regarded as the father of dark luxe Short Story. I am reminded of the short story, *The False*

Gems. It tells the story of Monsieur Lantin who met a young girl at a reception at the house of the second head of his department, and fell head over heels in love with her. They got married. He was unspeakably happy with her except that he found fault with only two of her tastes: Her love for the theatre, and her taste for imitation jewelry. Her friends frequently procured for her a box at the theatre, often for the first representations of the new plays; and her husband was obliged to accompany her to these entertainments which bored him excessively after his day's work at the office. After a time, Monsieur Lantin begged his wife to request some lady of her acquaintance to accompany her, and to bring her home after the theatre. She opposed this arrangement at first, but after much persuasion, finally consented, to the infinite delight of her husband. One evening, in winter, she had been to the opera, and returned home chilled through and through. The next morning she coughed, and eight days later, she died of inflammation of the lungs. Monsieur Lantin's despair was so great that his hair became white in one month. He wept unceasingly; his heart was broken as he remembered her smile, her voice, every charm of his dead wife. Time did not assuage his grief. To the last days of her life, she had continued to make purchases, bringing home new gems almost every evening, and he turned them over some time before finally deciding to sell the heavy necklace, which she seemed to prefer, and which, he thought, ought to be worth about six or seven francs; for it was of very fine workmanship, though only imitation. He visited the Jeweler Rue de la Paix and as soon as the proprietor glanced at the necklace, he could recognize and offered Eighteen thousand francs. Monsieur Lantin was dumfounded.

Dark luxe knows that villains often come with pretty faces. It knows that it's the craziest thing, but people can't stop. After all, heart-stopping envy of the luxe is the sincerest form of flattery.

The author's journey through the distorting mirror often leads to death via the greed and obscene.

Dark luxe sure can be perplexing, as Brahma, the well-respected luxe intellectual, makes clear in this wonderfully provocative book. There is, at the center of the book, his short stories, which he claims as fiction, examining the widely varying concepts of the ugliness of dark luxe down through time, referencing the insights of Maharajas, Zamindars and Princes. The second level of the book is made up of lengthy quotations that provide a visual perspective to the conversation.

Another dark luxe is the faux pas of the luxe. In fact, this market is worth several times more than the brand luxe. The episode in *Da Vinci Code* elucidates well the point. Professor Langdon and Sophie were inside the Depository Bank of Zurich when the French Police came enquiring. The police were blocking the street. They were smuggled inside the armoured bank car and locked inside. As they were leaving:

"Must have been hours ago. I'm driving all the way up to St. Thurial tonight. Cargo keys are already up there."

The agent made no response, his eyes probing as if trying to read Vernet's mind.

A drop of sweat was preparing to slide down Vernet's nose. "You mind?" he said, wiping his nose with his sleeve and motioning to the police car blocking his way. "I'm on a tight schedule."

"Do all the drivers wear Rolexes?" the agent asked, pointing to Vernet's wrist.

Vernet glanced down and saw the glistening band of his absurdly expensive watch peeking out from beneath the sleeve of his jacket. Merde. "This piece of shit? Bought it for twenty euro from a Taiwanese street vendor in St. Germain des Pres. I'll sell it to you for forty."

The agent paused and finally stepped aside. "No thanks. Have a safe trip."

Dark Luxe, it seems, is just more interesting than *Decoding Luxe*. At least, that's what I think now that I've read the book. Brahma may agree although he doesn't say that in so many words. Yet, in the opening pages of the book he writes:

"When we think of luxury, we only think of dazzle, but we never even touch upon the darkness that hides behind this luxe, thanks to us - humans. It is always about glam and glitz. Behind this razzle-dazzle, there is another life. A life filled with lust, hatred, jealousy, anger.

So these stories are purely a work of fiction, a figment of my imagination, and by no means has any intention to paint any luxury brand in a bad light or tarnish their pristine image. It merely captures the depths to which darkness can reach in human hearts."

The sensibility of the common speaker reveals that, whereas all the synonyms for de-luxe – distinctive, exquisite, heavenly, luxurious, opulent, savory, divine, flamboyant, ornate – could be conceived as a reaction of appreciation, almost all the synonyms for dark luxe contain a reaction of disgust, if not violent repulsion, horror, or fear.

We look at de-luxe, and we know it is a grace note of life. When we gaze on dark-luxe, we see the existence we share.

That's why, Brahma quotes :

"If you prick us, do we not bleed?
If you tickle us, do we not laugh?
If you poison us, do we not die?
And if you wrong us, shall we not revenge?

—*The Merchant of Venice,*
Act 3, Scene 1 by William Shakespeare

William Shakespeare may be called the "absolute acme of dark-luxe" — because he was an artist who blended de-and dark-luxe; beauty and ugliness as happens in nature, where individual beauties are never free of impurities, and both his works and his characters possess a wealth of these impurities.

I think there is a temptation to call the book 'a leer' due to its dark side. The look, the smile of the characters in the book could just as well be read as deep affection and delight. We would read it that way if he were a studly courtier, wouldn't we?

Though accompanying verbal snippets fight a losing battle with the images, this book is full of amazements.

Prof Aloke Kumar
Academician,
Author, Editor

What Dark Luxe *is all about*

Luxury has its origin in the word luxe, which means dazzle. So, whenever you think of luxury, it is always about razzle-dazzle; it is always about glam and glitz. The stuff dreams are made of. Dreams that only money can buy. And every bit of luxury exudes a shine that blinds the have-nots. This book is not about that glitter. This book is not about dreams either. No.

It is true that luxury creates a great divide between haves and have-nots. You either have it or you don't, or rather, you can either afford it, or you can't. No, this book is also not about that great social divide. Sorry, Mister Marx.

Behind this razzle-dazzle, there is another life. A life as real as that of the have-nots. A life filled with lust, hatred, jealousy, anger. A life very deprived, very starved. A life of horrors. A life of flesh and blood. But yes, a life to die for or rather kill for!

Luxury remains a silent witness to that darkness.

Dark Luxe is not about dreams, it is about nightmares. It is about those realities that safely hide behind the veil of luxe. These are tales of fiction from the darkest, bottomless pits of hell. These first-hand stories of horror are by stuff luxury is made of. Straight from their heart, leaving a trail of blood.

Disclaimer by the Author

I have been studying and commentating on luxury for years and have always been fascinated by luxury and brands. My first book *Decoding Luxe* is a homage to that dazzle.

When we think of luxury, we only think of dazzle, but we never even touch upon the darkness that hides behind this luxe, thanks to us – humans. It is always about glam and glitz. Behind this razzle-dazzle, there is another life. A life filled with lust, hatred, jealousy, anger.

So these stories are purely a work of fiction, a figment of my imagination, and by no means has any intention to paint any luxury brand in a bad light or tarnish their pristine image. It merely captures the depths to which darkness can reach in human hearts.

Luxury remains a silent witness to that darkness. So similarity, if any found, is purely co-incidental.

Mahul Brahma

Acknowledgements

I thank you, dear reader, from the bottom of my heart for choosing *Dark Luxe*. This book wouldn't have been possible without your love and support.

I am deeply indebted to Mr Amitabh Bachchan for his kind words of encouragement. They've meant the world to me.

I am thankful to Mr Ratan N. Tata for being such an inspiration and for making time to convey his best wishes again for my second book.

A big thanks to Bibek da (Debroy) for his wonderful foreword that has so beautifully captured the essence of the book.

Thanks to Himika, Kounteya and Alok da for writing such wonderful forewords.

I thank Mr Nirvik Singh (Chairman, Grey Advertising APAC) and Mr Jawhar Sircar (former CEO, Prasar Bharati) for your kind words and support.

A big thanks to Mr Harish Bhat (Author and Brand Custodian of Tata Sons) for his kind words and encouragement.

Thanks Mr TV Narendran (Global CEO and MD of Tata Steel) and Mr Sanjay Kapoor (MD of Genesis Luxury) for their encouragement for the book and for being a critic of my luxury columns.

I am thankful to Mr Vinaya Varma (CEO of mjunction), the board of directors of mjunction and the entire team of mj for encouraging me to pursue my passions.

Thank you Sumit, for rendering such wonderful illustrations. And thanks again Indranil for the lovely profile pic.

Thanks to all my friends and well-wishers for their support and blessings.

My heartfelt thanks to Arup and team Srishti Publishers for your continued support.

A special thanks, my better half Sabiya Sinha Roy. This book wouldn't have been possible without you.

And last but not the least, I am grateful to God Almighty for being so kind and generous, always.

I feel loved and blessed.

Mahul Brahma

A note from the author

Life of a luxury commentator (who can't afford luxury)

My first brush with luxury was with an inheritance – my grandfather's Omega Seamasters manual-wind mechanical watch. I was only fifteen then, so the sole reason for my attachment was because it was my grandfather's last gift. I started wearing it every day, despite a lot of resistance from my father. I realized the worth of the watch much later – eight years to be precise, when I walked into an Omega boutique in Mumbai. The manager was delighted to see this timepiece. He painstakingly explained to me how precious the watch is – the movements, the elegance of a mechanical watch, and the story behind the watch and what it can be worth to a collector. For the first time I started taking interest in luxury brands.

That watch had, unwittingly since my teens, made me very comfortable with luxury.

A few years later, I started writing on luxury and editing a luxury supplement. Later, with my columns, I explored the various facets of luxury. Unfortunately, I realized there wasn't any literature available, even globally, on what constitutes luxe. Most of the books were glorified catalogues. This compelled me to write by first book *Decoding Luxe* to give readers a holistic picture of what this animal called luxury is all about.

As a luxury commentator, it is easy to connect with the custodians as well as owners of the large luxury brands globally; they are happy to open the doors for you, give you a taste, and an experience of luxe. You are touched by it. I have been experiencing luxury so that I can share an honest and sincere story with my readers. I feel blessed that although I can't afford luxury, I can make my readers experience luxe through my commentary.

My first editor Jojo at *The Economic Times* taught me that as a journalist, you can't be overwhelmed. You have to be neutral and just, keeping the readers' best interests in your mind. So when I was a business editor, to me, a significant amount which was worthy of coverage in my paper would not be less than a few hundreds of crores. The bigger the figure the better. So even figures in tens of crores would be 'small' and 'insignificant'. I used to later have a hearty laugh as to how I just look down upon such figures, which otherwise, are huge. Blame it on the editor's hat I was wearing.

So when I experience luxury, these figures and price tags fail to overwhelm me. I do not look at it from the perspective of affordability or ownership or awe. I look at it from the sheer sense of responsibility as a commentator towards my readers.

So, while sipping a vintage Dom Pérignon, I can only think of myself as James Bond as I tell you very critically, "My dear girl, there are some things that just aren't done, such as drinking Dom Perignon '53 above the temperature of 38 degrees Fahrenheit. That's as bad as listening to the Beatles without earmuffs!"

My readers, *Dark Luxe* explores a side that is not known or talked about; the murmurs safely hidden behind the walls of fortresses.

Happy reading!

Prologue

The Dark Life of Luxe

*Deep into that darkness peering,
long I stood there, wondering, fearing,
doubting, dreaming dreams no mortal ever dared
to dream before.*

—Edgar Allan Poe

During my early days of luxury journalism, so much was I consumed with the dazzle that I couldn't even imagine there could exist another side to it – a darker side, a side which should not be spoken of. It was much later I started exploring the dark life of luxury. Looking deep into that darkness, I started dreaming dreams no mortal ever dared to dream before.

I realized, with dazzle, comes the darkness – Yin and Yang. It is the world's way of maintaining the order. After a lot of research and interviews, I came across shocking tales of death, blood and gore associated with luxury. I realized we are only limited by our imagination to fathom the extent a man can go to in his pursuit of darkness.

Luxe or dazzle acts as a cover, a shield to keep this dark life of us humans at bay.

From the glossy magazine pages with 'price on request' tag, *Dark Luxe* takes you, dear readers, to the other end of the spectrum.

These horror stories are pure work of fiction and are crafted as tales from the proverbial horse's mouth. They are shared (in the stories) by the most sought-after and elite products that the crème-de-la-crème brands showcase to their exclusive patrons.

These are the stories that are buried deep in the Mediterranean or in the uninhabited sanctum-sanctorum of our hearts.

These stories tell you the tale of how we humans are all the same in our core, dominated by the seven deadly sins – lust, gluttony, greed, sloth, wrath, envy and pride – in various permutations and combinations.

Whether it is the Princess Cut Tiffany ring or the Rolls Royce Phantom, the Rolex watch or the luxury yacht or a Dom Perignon vintage champagne – all of them will share their tales as a silent witness that are far from the dazzle they exude.

These short stories about the dark life of luxe are figments of my imagination, but not limited by it alone.

Death of a Phantom

If you prick us, do we not bleed?
If you tickle us, do we not laugh?
If you poison us, do we not die?
And if you wrong us, shall we not revenge?

—*The Merchant of Venice,* Act 3,
Scene 1, by William Shakespeare

There is a saying that I run on reputation. I am the Phantom of reputation. I am the Rolls Royce Phantom. I am the mark of class, snobbery – the ultimate in luxury. When I drive down the road, people bow with respect and awe.

When I was brought to London, I was treated like a king. I have seen my guards not allowing commoners to even get close to me. And then one day I saw a sharp-looking young Indian in very English attire walking into the store and looking straight at me. It was a very appreciative look. Suddenly, Luke, the store attendant very rudely asked him to leave the store. "Sir, I will request you to leave immediately, otherwise I will have to call security."

The Indian was red with anger, and shouted, "How dare you speak to me like that? Do you have any idea who you are speaking to?"

Luke raised his voice and made him leave in seething anger. I felt so bad for him.

The next day, I came to know that a Maharaja from India was coming to see us. And if he liked us, he would take all six of us to his kingdom. I was happy that I would be a royal ride, befitting my stature. The store was all decked up with a red carpet rolled out for the Maharaja.

And then I saw him, in all his grand attire, walking the red carpet, ushered by the manager Mr Jerry himself. The face looked familiar. He came and stood in front of me, looking straight at me.

I now could recognize it was the young Indian who had been asked to leave this store the past day, standing in front of me in his finery.

Without wasting a minute, he ordered his manager to buy me and paid even the shipping changes upfront. Jerry meekly came forward to apologize,

"I am sorry, Your Highness, the attendant Luke could not recognize you yesterday."

Luke profusely apologized. The Maharaja smirked, didn't say a word to him. Little did I know what was in store for me.

I was shipped for India within a week.

And it seemed like ages when I finally reached the shores of India. During the 1920-30s, India was one of the largest consuming nations for the RR Phantom.

It took five hours for the royal attendants to make me ready for the Maharaja. I had never seen such beautiful decorations – all adorned in gold, exquisitely hand-crafted. I was feeling like a king who was getting ready to greet another king. A royal meet.

It was sunset, and the tint of the orange sun had given an ethereal glow to my golden costume. The Maharaja walked in. He stood before me for long, just admiring my royalty.

He ordered something in his local dialect, which I could not understand. He looked at me. He smiled and then left abruptly. He would not take me for a drive? Why was I decked up then? May be he didn't because it was dark. He'd probabaly take me out in the morning. I couldn't sleep that night.

The palace was on top of a hill, within a high fortress. There were dangerous edges, which fell very sharply to the seemingly bottomless ravine. The next morning when I was expecting the Maharaja, the attendants came to me again. They changed my attire and dressed me up in another royal golden suit. Yes, the mighty Maharaja would drive me around his kingdom now. I really wanted to explore his kingdom.

After hours of patient waiting, I was finally ready. To my surprise, a man in a white local dress with a turban came up to me and started my engine. You commoner, how dare you drive this majestic Phantom?

He drove me down the hill through the terrible roads for twenty kilometers, reaching a village market. A crowd immediately gathered around me, admiring my royalty. Then he suddenly killed the engine and jumped on my bonnet. Are you crazy, you commoner? You will be punished for insulting me. The Maharaja will never spare you.

The commoner shouted something to the crowd in a local dialect, after which there was pin drop silence. Not a single villager was uttering a word. They looked confused. Then they all went away. The commoner got down and opened all my doors and trunk wide. In a few minutes, I saw the villagers coming back with things in the hands. Before I could realize what was happening, one old man threw what he was carrying inside me, on the backseat. It was garbage. The next ten minutes felt like an eternity. I couldn't believe what was happening. All the villagers were filling the mighty Phantom up with garbage.

Why would the Maharaja do such a thing to the mighty Phantom? Why would a Maharaja not respect the Phantom?

It was dusk when we reached the palace. The entire garbage of the village was inside me. I was made to wait for the Maharaja to come. The commoner stood by my side. I was stationed at an edge, a beautiful edge which led straight down a few hundred feet if you were not careful.

The Maharaja walked in and stood on the edge. The grin on his face visible. I know this grin – this is a grin of victory, of triumph.

The Maharaja told me he loved this spot. He loved it as it was an edge of mystery, an edge that separated life and death. He stood there, still, enjoying the setting sun. He then looked at me. The humiliated Phantom – the garbage bearer.

He shouted to me, "Make no mistake, this will be your routine till your last day and then you will be sold as scrap. And if I feel like, I will throw you down this hill right now, you filthy garbage carrier. You piece of garbage!"

The Maharaja started laughing. His laughter echoed in the hills.

I am the Phantom, the car of the elite, and this is my fate?

I cried silently. I was standing still in the shadows, watching the laughing Maharaja, just a few feet away. My driver was grinning as well.

I couldn't take the insults anymore. I flashed my headlamps on the Maharaja. The strong lights blinded him for a moment. He shouted at my clueless driver.

I hit the accelerator hard. My 624 horsepower engine roared. In a blink, I hit the Maharaja and threw him off the edge into the depth of the hills.

I needed to see the 'garbage' fall. I enjoyed his warm blood on me as I fell down the hill along with him.

He had forgotten, after all, I was the Phantom.

Life of an Empress

It boils within
slowly poisoning all that it touches
Corrupting all that is within
it has now reached a new level
A level I never thought existed
for it has boiled over everything
everything I have
Everything I've worked to keep
for I am now totally corrupted
drowning in poison
The poison of my life
the poison you all help create
The poison that has been growing within me
Anger
Anger is that poison.

—'Anger' by Scarlet

My day starts in the middle of the night. I am the empress of the deep blue seas. I am the luxe, I am the dazzle. I am the aspiration. I am over three hundred feet long and can go as fast as seventy knots. I am what dreams are made of. I am The Empress.

I belong to a King. I loved the Mediterranean Sea, just like my King. He used to take his beautiful wives and girlfriends out, three or four at a time, and spend weeks on the high seas with them. They used to have fun, swim naked in the clear seas and make love; sometimes in pairs, sometimes all of them together. I used to love watching them sunbathing on my deck. They loved me too.

It was only with his special girlfriend Tatania, a Russian supermodel, he used to sail by himself. Even his bodyguard was not allowed when Tatania was on board. They were madly in love, I could see. They used to spend sleepless nights under the moon, holding hands and each other. I know when it is love. I had never seen this love in the eyes of my King for any of his wives or other girlfriends. It was just for Tatania and her green eyes. The King loved to play with her red hair. She used to dress up for him occasionally, but mostly in her birthday suit. So gorgeous, so dazzling, so perfect, so smooth – just like I am.

The King was very possessive of Tatania. He loved her every time he saw her on a magazine or on a hoarding. Unfortunately, he also hated her every time he saw her on a magazine or on a hoarding. He hated imagining how other men ogled at her pictures in a bikini or a swimsuit. Made him go mad. He had been trying to convince her to leave modeling for the past one year, but Tatania loved modeling. She loved the attention and she loved the ogles too. She, more than anything, loved her identity. She had an identity as a model and hated to be reduced to a title of the King's mistress. They had argued over this issue earlier, but love had conquered all. They were too much in love with each other.

Tatania wanted to surprise him. She was featured in a magazine where the world's most sought-after photographer had profiled her in his experimental shoot. The King was so happy that he kissed her and started to look through the pictures. Suddenly, he stumbled upon a photo where she had posed nude. The King was furious. I had never seen him this angry; he always was playful and joyous. His eyes were shot red.

And then came that dreaded night. The darkest of the dark nights. Managing his anger has never been his strength. He was drinking his usual Dom Pérignon '52. But there was a difference. He had already finished five bottles and was now on the sixth Dom. Tatania was very excited as the feature had been widely appreciated and she had cemented her position as a top model. She just could not understand why the King would react this way.

"You whore!" the King shouted. "You have no shame? How can you pose nude? You are sleeping with this bastard, aren't you? I am not man enough for you? How many men do you need? Everyone saw you naked, you bitch."

While the King was shouting, tears rolled down his eyes. His anger and his emotions were taking the better of him.

Tatania was screaming and crying. I could only understand that the intensity of the fight was increasing and that the King was losing his head.

The moonlight was shining on her face. She was so beautiful. The moonlight was reflecting on her skin, but I was missing her smile.

The King became silent, still crying, which got louder and louder, and looking at Tatania, her pristine beauty. "How could you do this to me, you bitch?" the King's voice shattered the momentary silence of the sea. In a blink, she was on the floor of the deck, covered in a strange concoction of blood and champagne. The King was holding the broken Dom Pérignon '52, blood dripping from the broken glass. Both were still. Everything suddenly went silent, even the sea.

The moon kept shining on her pristine white body, which was still warm, covered in blood. She was still. The King, after regaining his stupor, realized what he had done. He threw the blood-soaked broken bottle of Dom into the sea, and started screaming and crying. He sat on the deck, shaking her, shouting her name, crying.

"Please Tatania, don't leave me. Please don't go. I am so sorry baby. I love you baby."

He was crying and screaming. No one could hear him, except me, The Empress.

In the next one hour, time stood still. It seemed like eternity. The King was holding his beloved close to his heart, kissing her.

After another eternity, just before dawn, the King stood up. He lifted Tatania in his arms, kissed her goodbye and threw her in the deep blue Mediterranean Sea.

I miss Tatania. I miss the happy King.

After one day, I reached the shore.

I was docked. For days, for months. I used to think about Tatania. I used think about my King. The great time we had. I missed the seas, the fun, the laughter, the happiness. Not a day went by that I didn't think about that dreaded night when I witnessed the murder of love.

And then one fine day, I saw my new owner. He was not a king by lineage, but he was my King, the King of happy times. He took me back on the seas. He loved me. He also loved to party with pretty girls. He loved Monacco and most of his parties were hosted there. The Mediterranean Sea, the Caribbean and the Indian Ocean were his favourite. I was again the host of happy times with beauty and fun.

A few years went by with the merrymaking.

The Empress was back as the symbol of luxe in the high seas.

I have been docked again, for months now. I haven't set sail in a while. I haven't seen my new King in a while. No parties. No beauty. No fun. No happy times. I am getting a little nervous. I really pray everything is fine with him. The Empress loves her King.

Death of Dom '52

*I saw grief drinking a cup of sorrow and called out,
'It tastes sweet, does it not?'*

*'You've caught me,' grief answered, 'and you've
ruined my business. How can I sell sorrow, when
you know it's a blessing?*

—Rumi

An affair that dates back to the fifties. An affair to remember. An affair with the most stylish and dynamic 'double O'. The name is Bond, James Bond. And he is with Her Majesty's Secret Service. While I was born in 1952, the story began in 1955, with Ian Fleming's book *Moonraker*. It was in this book that Bond was introduced to me – a vintage Dom Pérignon, by the wine-waiter at Blades during the dinner with M. Our love affair started that very night and it was captured beautifully in celluloid.

I hate it when he simply ignores me and lets me get warm. I like the cold. I like him to take care of me. I don't know why he forgets every time that love making without me, will have no vintage. I make his love making timeless. Even when I am not half done, he just forgets about me. He knows if I get warmer than 38 degrees Fahrenheit, I lose my class, my taste. But still he just ignores me.

But I know Bond loves me. He has always been biased towards people who appreciate my vintage. "Any man who drinks Dom Pérignon '52 can't be all bad," he always says.

He knows my rich heritage. I am not like his easy-pickup 'Bond girls'. And no Vodka Martini, whether shaken or stirred, can ever replace my luxe. I need appreciation and pampering. I derive my name, my lineage, from the great 17th century monk and cellar master at the Benedictine Abbey in Hautvillers. He is the pioneer in champagne-making and made me what I am.

My creator, my God.

I am the drink of the King of Kings. I am a work of art for connoisseurs and collectors. I am auctioned at Christie's. Since my vintage 1921, I am the undisputed luxe in the world of wines.

If you recall, I was served at the wedding of gorgeous Princess D.

This story is about Omar, who loved me, the '52. So everywhere he went, he would take me with him. He simply did not touch anything except me. And yes, his women. Just me and his women. Just like Commander Bond. I was there in his private jet, in his Rolls Royces and Limousines, and in his yacht. His yacht and private jet were the hot seats for his private parties, where he was the only alfa male and all women – his wives, his mistresses, his muses, supermodels and actresses. Always in sumptuous permutations and combinations. I was a witness to all his love makings.

This happened one night when Omar was down a few bottles, much more than his usual. He was holding me by my neck, half empty. I could see he was very upset. Shouting and screaming at a girl. She was beautiful, like a supermodel. She was crying but the things she was saying was somehow making Omar more and more upset and angry. The biggest weakness of Omar was his anger. It is an inheritance, a legacy, runs in the royal veins.

Suddenly, he snapped and smashed me on the girl's head. In a blink, I was broken. My broken pieces were stuck inside the skull of the girl, who just dropped dead. Omar was still holding my neck and the remaining of the broken '52. For the first time, I tasted blood. The blood of an innocent girl. A beautiful girl, who was killed by me. In the moonlight I could see how beautiful she was.

Omar stood still for a few minutes and then started crying and screaming, realizing what he had done. He immediately looked at me and threw me into the Mediterranean Sea.

This is the end, my friend.

Life of a Princess

Diamonds are forever, they are all I need to please me
They can stimulate and tease me
They won't leave in the night
I've no fear that they might desert me
Diamonds are forever, hold one up and then caress it
Touch it, stroke it and undress it
I can see ev'ry part, nothing hides in the heart to hurt me
I don't need love, for what good will love do me?

—'Diamonds are Forever'.
From the 007 movie, sung by Shirley Bassey

It has been exactly six months and ten days since I've seen her. I've been left in the cold. She used to look at me all the time; there was so much love in her eyes. She used to kiss me every time she set her deep blue eyes on me.

It was not a goodbye, it couldn't have been a goodbye. I am sure it was not.

Bethany, where are you? Come back. Love me just the way you used to, always. Come, kiss me Bethany. Please don't abandon me. I miss you.

James loved Bethany. I know how hard it was for him to bring me home. But he never flinched. He loved Bethany so much.

What a day it was – the most beautiful day of my life. The way Bethany was happy to see me. Oh! The way she kissed me.

We have been bringing smiles to couples since 1886, when Charles Lewis Tiffany launched the Tiffany Setting to highlight the fire and beauty of a solitaire diamond, introducing the world to the engagement ring as we know it today. Mr Tiffany was called 'King of Diamonds' and he came to the city of New York in 1837 to open his first store.

Yes, hello, I am a Princess Cut Tiffany engagement ring.

I am proud of my lineage.

I am the messenger of love. I bring couples together. I add luxe to their lives.

I remember James used to come almost every day to my home, the boutique. He used come and spend a long time just looking at me. I know I don't come cheap, but if it is for his special someone, cost should be the last thing on his mind. James is a hardworking upper middle class lad. I know he has taken a bank loan for me. But that's okay; having me is not easy.

I remember the day when Bethany came to the store for the first time. She was so beautiful. She was in a pink flowing gown, her golden hair cascading down her beautiful neck. It was love at first sight. I slipped onto her finger perfectly. Just like a perfect match. I remember her first kiss – her lips red as a rose, so soft.

I finally went with James to his home. Every time Bethany used to visit him, she always used to look at me with her eager beautiful blue eyes, dying to take me with her. She used to call me 'Princess' after my cut.

And the day arrived. Finally. Bethany was in her red Valentino gown and James in his Tom Ford tuxedo. James went down on his knees and popped the question. It is rare for the girl to say no when it is me on the other side. James gently slipped me on her beautiful finger.

Bethany kissed me first. Then they kissed – a long and lingering kiss. She was so happy. Her smile was shining more than I was.

It was also the day when I saw Bethany' college friend and James' colleague Lara. She seemed more interested in me than the engagement ceremony. I don't blame her. I am beautiful and have such an effect on girls.

Six months passed. These were the happiest months that I have ever spent. The two love-birds were so much into each other. I could see the love in their eyes.

They decided to get married after three months. I was so happy for them.

Bethany became busy with the arrangements and bookings.

One fine day, when James was in office, Lara came to visit Bethany. She was crying. Bethany comforted her, gave her some water.

Lara said, "Bethany, you need to know something. I thought I'd never share this secret with you, but I need to tell you this."

She continued, "James raped me."

Bethany slapped Lara and asked her to leave.

Lara requested her to at least hear her out.

Lara pulled out the cell phone from her purse and showed Bethany James' text, sent the day before, threatening to rape her and beat her again if she uttered a word to Bethany. Lara, with tears in her eyes, narrated her story.

The incident happened one month ago, when both of them were on an office tour. It was way past midnight. James was drunk and forced himself into Lara's hotel room. He hit her, abused her and then raped her. Over and over again, till Lara lost consciousness.

When she regained her senses, James was gone. She could barely walk. She was so scared and injured that she didn't know what to do. For the next few hours, seething in unbearable pain, she just cried. She was too scared even to go to a hospital. She spent the next two days locked up in the hotel room with her only companion – pain.

A week later, she summoned the courage to confront James. He responded with a threat about her job. Yes, James was senior to her and could have gotten her fired. Lara needed the job, she couldn't risk it. Even after what happened.

But James grew insecure that Lara would tell Bethany, may be in a moment of some emotional upheaval. The threat of a job was not powerful enough to contain that. So two nights ago, he visited Lara's home. Sloshed.

He again beat her up and then raped her. This time threatening to rape her whenever he pleased. Soon after, he came inside her.

He left immediately.

Lara said, "He will kill me, Bethany. I am so scared."

Bethany knew about James cutting his office trip short. Ever since he had been back, he always seemed irritated and angry, even shouting at times. Not his normal self. He did come home sloshed two night ago, almost at dawn. Bethany was blaming herself for this recent change in James' behaviour because she was always tense and at times crazy with all the wedding arrangements. Lara's story started to fall in place.

For the first time, Bethany's tears fell on me. Everything changed.

Her smile was wiped clean.

Bethany looked again at the threat message.

James. How could he? He is such a gentle person. He loves me so much.

Suddenly Lara said something that shook Bethany's faith in James, completely. "After James was done beating me and raping me, he burnt my inner thigh with cigarette stubs. See!

She lifted her dress and showed the butt marks.

Bethany remembered the night two months ago when they had had a fight. James had been drunk. He did force himself on her in the night and made love to her against her will, but no, it was not rape. And when he was done, he burnt her inner thighs too with cigarette butts. He kept kissing her so she let that pass as an aberration. But Bethany could not recognize her fiancé that night. He had seemed like a stranger.

Bethany went silent. She asked Lara to leave.

I first felt her tears. She didn't tell James a thing. She was dead silent.

The next day, I could suddenly taste her warm blood. It was oozing from her left wrist... from the veins. I was helpless. I couldn't even cry for help.

I was covered in blood, I could not see anything.

After a while, James separated me from Bethany, and put me in his pocket. I was still covered in her blood. The next day, he washed me and put me away in his drawer. I know she had been taken to the hospital.

Time passed. Days, then a month and then two. Soon six months and ten days had passed. Suddenly, the drawer opened. Yes, my Bethany, I want to go back to you, your Princess. But it was James. He took me out and turned me over to... no... but why was he handing me over to Lara? Had he gone completely insane? I was Bethany's Princess.

Lara slowly slid me over her finger. I could see her smirk, the message was loud and clear, "You are my Princess now".

Death of a Trunk

I have to do it, I have to do it. I have to keep my reason in mind. I won't say out loud what my reason is, but I have to do it. But I won't shed any of her blood or scar that beautiful skin, whiter than snow and smooth as the finest marble. But she's got to die, or she'll cheat on other men. Put out the light of the candle, and then put out the light of her heart. If I extinguish the candle, I can light it again if I regret it. But once I kill you, you beautiful, fake woman, I do not know the magic that could bring you back. When I've plucked this rose, I can't make it grow again; it will have no choice but to wither and die.

Act 5 Scene 2, *Othello* by William Shakespeare

I am sinking. I don't have the power to struggle. I feel there is no life in me. As the cold Mediterranean Sea slowly engulfs me, inside me wrapped in white satin... is... flesh and blood. Yes. A beautiful girl, just twenty-one.

The boyfriend was the Nawab of Jannatabad. He had just turned twenty-five last month. He was a fine lad otherwise, the only problem – drugs. Well, there was another problem – jealousy. His mother never bothered about him after the death of her husband, the previous Nawab, ten years ago. She had her own affairs to manage and she kept herself busy with that.

His girlfriend Sonia was the only one who loved him. I always thought he loved her too.

They used to travel the world in his private jet. Nawab had a friend who used to own a huge yacht named The Empress. They loved partying on the yacht in exotic locales across the globe. I always accompanied them. Nawab loved me. Took care of me. He had branded me with his initials – NJ.

Sonia and Nawab were in their usual presidential suite at their Monte Carlo hotel and casino The Royale. They were madly in love.

But Nawab was a jealous man and insecure about his relationship with Sonia. He suspected Sonia was cheating on him. He had trust issues. All along this trip, they had been fighting. Nawab had been shouting at her. But today, they had been mostly silent with intermittent bouts of fighting.

It was way past midnight and Nawab was high on cocaine. It was a much higher dose than his usual quota. Sonia was asleep in the other room. They have been living like this since they started their fight. Visions of Sonia having sex with Fawad Khan, her best friend the singer, kept flashing before him. The more he saw these visions, more the jealousy burned. And the more he snorted. The more he kept losing his senses. He pulled out his pistol and went straight to Sonia's room. He forced himself on her. He pressed the muzzle hard against Sonia's navel. He was on her. She kept resisting and screaming. He didn't listen. He never listened.

"Bitch, I can't let that bastard fuck you. Only I can. Do you hear that? You are only mine, you bitch!" he kept on shouting.

The Nawab started beating her. She tried to resist, but he was too strong and completely out of his senses. He came inside her and in his orgasmic ecstasy, the pistol roared. I heard Sonia scream and everything suddenly went silent.

Yes. I was a witness to the crime.

The night in white satin was filled with her blood. She was on the bed – naked, bruised and still warm

Nawab threw the pistol away. He didn't even realize what he had just done.

He had raped her and then murdered her. His Sonia was dead.

The Nawab hugged her and started to cry. An hour or so went by.

He picked up the phone and called his friend, King Omar. He was in his yacht The Empress, which was docked at the Monte Carlo shore.

"Don't worry, I am sending my trusted man. He will clean the mess. You leave immediately and come to my yacht. My man will handle everything," Omar said.

Nawab kissed Sonia a final goodbye. The last lingering kiss. For the first time, she did not kiss him back. He covered her with the white satin sheet, picked up his pistol and left.

An hour later, a tall dark figure entered the room. His face was cold. He carefully checked the suite and finally reached Sonia's room. He saw Sonia lying cold under the satin sheet. He removed the sheet. He stood still, admiring her flawless naked body.

He realized he was aroused. He slowly unzipped his trousers.

What is he trying to do? You bastard, stop, you pervert.

He abused and raped Sonia's corpse. He smiled as he cleaned her blood from his body. Such a cold smile, it sent chills down my spine.

He looked at me. He put me on the bed.

He wrapped Sonia with the satin sheets. He then crammed her inside me. Somehow her lithe body fitted inside me.

I was dragged to his car and placed inside safely.

I am the mighty Louis Vuitton trunk or 'malle,' in French, with a legacy dating back to 1858. Vuitton introduced the Damier canvas in 1888 and I am the rare pattern – dark red dots over a dark brown background and white checker. Inside me is the 'marque L. Vuitton déposée', where Sonia is resting peacefully.

I now know my destiny – Sonia and I will decay together. I know he was heading for the sea. Within ten minutes, I could hear the waves smashing against the shore. I was transferred to a small yacht and taken deep into the sea.

I know the time has come.

My new home with Sonia – the Mediterranean Sea.

Till decay do us part!

Life of a Logo

Was this the face that launch'd a thousand ships,
And burnt the topless towers of Ilium?
Sweet Helen, make me immortal with a kiss.
Her lips suck forth my soul: see where it flies!
Come, Helen, come, give me my soul again.
Here will I dwell, for heaven is in these lips,
And all is dross that is not Helena.
I will be Paris, and for love of thee,
Instead of Troy, shall Wittenberg be sack'd;
And I will combat with weak Menelaus,
And wear thy colours on my plumed crest;
Yea, I will wound Achilles in the heel,
And then return to Helen for a kiss.

— 'Doctor Faustus' by Christopher Marlowe

Flaunters belong to a category of luxury consumers who are in love with logos. Their primary area of appreciation is the logo of the luxury brands that they can flaunt. So, to them, more than the craftsmanship or legacy of the brand, what matters is the logo. They pay for value-for-label. As long as a logo has a flaunt quotient, they will keep loving it, irrespective of anything else. This behaviour is very different from connoisseurs. The latter breed is more concerned with the story behind the brand, the craftsmanship and with things which they can appreciate and savour. It can be a single malt or a cigar, what matters to them is not the label, but what that label or logo represents. For example, it is not about flaunting the Dom Pérignon bottle like a flaunter, to a connoisseur it is about appreciating the vintage – its smell, its taste and its lingering beauty.

I am a luxury brand logo. You can call me L, and this is my story with my lover – the flaunter Happy.

With Happy, it was love at first sight. He first saw me in *Forbes* in an airport lounge. It was an advertisement of my scarf, worn by a Hollywood actress. But that day I lured him more than the seductress in the print.

He secretly tore the page, folded it neatly and placed it inside his wallet.

I think he found my curves sexier than Angie's.

Happy was never into labels. He was a simple man in his thirties with a simple, average job and a mundane life. An average

Joe with an average life. The biggest labels he had ever used were just premium brands.

I introduced him to the real world – the world of luxury.

With me in his pocket, suddenly, he felt a sense of awe.

I made him visit my boutique and make a purchase that was way above his budget. I told him not to be afraid. He thought he never needed a scarf, such a fool. You need it to flaunt me – the L logo, you idiot!

The next day at his workplace, everyone looked at him differently. He secretly told me his colleagues were green with envy. He loved that. I encouraged him to keep the envy alive.

Happy, my happy man, started frequenting luxury boutiques. He started appreciating the high life. A life less ordinary. He started enjoying the fact that he could make people jealous by flaunting the luxury brand logos. It gave him a sense of superiority to all these 'mere mortals' who flaunt their mid-to-premium labels. He felt ashamed that he was once a part of this very category that he so despised.

After all, the brands that Happy was flaunting are used by the greats – Hollywood stars, billionaires, rockstars, industrialists, barons, and the richie rich of the world. He is a part of that legacy – the elite club of Brand L owners. And everybody should acknowledge that.

As a dutiful lover, I supported him throughout his journey in this world of logos. I loved the way he used to flaunt the logos at every party, every event, in fact every occasion. Happy distinctly stood out and made an impression. He had now started noticing others who were also flaunting their logos. They compared and talked about what was new and what else they had.

In an office party, suddenly he realized that he shared his love for me 'Brand L' with the company's Vice President AKG. During his entire tenure, he never had an opportunity to even say 'good morning' or 'hi' to him. AKG spotted his scarf logo and walked up to him. He could not believe his eyes. It was like a dream. They started chatting about their love for me, amid talks about other brands. All his colleagues were green with jealousy, again, and Happy loved the expression on their faces. Now Happy and AKG were connected via WhatsApp!

His love for me increased that day onwards.

Happy was in a whole new world. A world where he had a rich legacy.

A year went by in happiness.

But there were times I saw Happy sad. He became sad if people failed to notice his new label. He felt bad if someone pointed out that he had worn his Armani jacket earlier or if someone was sporting a more expensive or latest version than his.

One day, someone was ringing the doorbell madly. Happy opened the door and there stood two very rude men. Happy recognized them and went pale. Happy said, "Please do not worry, give me a month and I will pay the dues. I promise." One of the men said, "Happy ji, we will come again if you fail to pay by the fifteenth. And we will be forced to take action. And next time, please take our calls."

They were collection agents of his credit card company and of the bank he had taken a personal loan from. In the next two weeks, more such people started frequenting and tormenting Happy. Happy's debt had gone into lakhs.

It was over a year that he had paid the 'minimum amount due' for his credit cards. He had failed to pay even that amount. Just the interests had risen to uncomfortable levels.

Happy always used to look at me and the other logos and feel happy. And when he used to get a chance to flaunt them, he would be very happy again.

You are worth every trouble, Happy used to tell me.

Another month passed by, and with every passing day, Happy became more and more terrified to take calls or answer the door. He had missed the payments, again.

He could not arrange for the funds. He was lost completely. He had nowhere to go. Even his friends refused to loan him funds.

He has started receiving threats from the agents.

Happy had stopped going to office for the past three weeks. He had stopped meeting friends. He had stopped calling his mother back home. Somehow his mother sensed something was wrong and came to visit him. She repeatedly asked him what had happened, but he just pretended everything was fine. He was just not keeping well, he told her.

Things were not well visibly. Happy was not happy anymore. He was scared, terrified and under constant fear of the agents.

Two days later, the doorbell rang. Happy's mother opened the door. Two men pushed her aside and reached for Happy in the bedroom. They beat him to pulp and told him he would not be spared the next time. On their way out, they destroyed most of Happy's precious collection of labels and logos.

When they left, Happy managed to pick himself up and came to the drawing room. He saw his mother on the floor, unconscious, blood on her forehead. When they had pushed past her, her head had hit the table's corner.

Happy started crying. He started shouting and screaming. "What have I done? What have I done? I lost everything, I lost everything."

We were all on the floor, some broken. He sat down and touched us. I could taste his tears and blood. He took me and rushed to the bedroom and closed the door from inside.

An hour later when his mother gained consciousness, she looked for Happy, but couldn't find him. She rushed for the bedroom. It was bolted from inside. She shouted his name. There was silence on the other side of the door. She tried to push the door open, to break it. But couldn't.

She ran to call the neighbour. After a lot of effort, the neighbour was finally able to break the door.

Happy was gone. He was hanging from a cheap ceiling fan with a scarf. Embroidered on it was his first love, his first owned logo – L.

Death of a Logo

I too like to take revenge
on those who hated me,
badly treated me,
berated me
and grated
my tender feelings cruelly.

I keep my weapons ready,
for accidental accost, if any
to confront them...
yes...with open arms,
glowing smile,
gracious visage
and lastly
with a heartfelt embrace!

    —*My Revenge* by Sathya Narayana

When David first saw me, it was love at first sight. He couldn't believe that he had created me so perfectly. I represent all the virtues of the brand so impeccably. Yes, I was perfect. I was the logo that the luxury brand needed to make an impression and charge a higher premium. It was on me to bring back the golden days of the brand.

I pity my predecessor, but honestly, she really looked ugly. I wonder why David, the brand custodian, had ever bothered creating her. Was he blind? And the brand had suffered because of that wrong choice. They needed to create me as the saviour of the luxury label. And now, I had to clear her mess.

Logo rules.

Old (logo) was a loser, from the first day. She never understood the brand. She never represented what the brand stood for. She was a mistake, a big mistake. David's biggest perhaps. But she was treated like a queen for almost two years. She was on display on all luxury shopping meccas – Upper 5th Avenue (USA), Causeway Bay (HK), New Bond Street (UK) and Prime A (UAE).

It was all going well for the first ten months – the investment time. But when it was time for payback, she fell short of promise. Two financial quarters went by with stagnant sales and then suddenly the brand pull loosened and sales started plummeting. It was a failure waiting to happen. I just blame David.

But not to worry now, your New is here. I am the Diva that will take the brand to its pinnacle.

David needs to understand that you need to be a snob, and not inclusive. Unless you make people feel small and excluded, they will never aspire for you. Look at me, I am like modern art; you will never be able to understand me fully. And this mystery will generate awe and interest. You need to be esoteric, obtuse. My predecessor was too inclusive and clear for everyone to quickly understand. And forget. That's precisely why people lost interest.

And six months have passed.

The management has started showing disappointment. They want the sales figures to pick up right now. Have they gone crazy? The entire brand campaign and logo unveiling just got over in four countries. They need to invest more in me. How can they seek results now? They gave my predecessor ten months straight. David needs to hold his ground. I can see the transformation is very near, but at least give me that time. I just need a little more push. Campaigns in India and China will bring in the change, I swear. David, don't yield to their pressure. Stay on, my friend, keep fighting for me. I promise you I will not let you down.

It's all because of that bitch Old. She was such a colossal failure, and for her, the management has lost faith in the logo.

One night in his cabin, David was with us. Drinking.

For the first time, I could sense disappointment in him.

He had made crystal figurines of me and also of that bitch Old. He always used to hold me and speak to me. Very privately. Here, in his cabin. He gave me the respect of his creation. I know he wanted answers from me. And I am certain he could hear my response.

David told me, "I think I was wrong, New. I thought being outlandish and esoteric will be the key. I was wrong. M (his boss and the owner of the luxury fashion brand) told me that it is alienating people."

"Are you crazy? Just give me at least two more months and see what happens. Your idea was just brilliant. I am brilliant. I am what the brand needed, M needs to be told that. Loud and clear."

"You were right. Do you hear me, David?"

A month passed by. The India and China campaigns were postponed indefinitely due to budget constraints. The sales in the US and the UK high streets have not picked up. I am certain they will. They are bound to pick up.

They are not picking up right now because the marketing team is a dud. They love to blame me and my poor David. Had they done their bit, I would have been able to show my magic. I told David later that night.

We were talking every night. He was exceeding his usual quota of his favourite Suntory Yamazaki 18-Year-Old with every passing night. He was fighting with the management every day, but I could see him wearing out.

One night, I was shocked. Instead of me, he picked up Old and started talking to her. Can you even imagine, he told that bitch, "I think I was wrong. I rushed in removing you. It was not for you that the sales were not picking up; it was because of external issues and the stupid marketing team. I am sorry. I should have given you some more time. Even M told me this today. He had asked me to drop the campaign altogether and get new creatives done with you. M said people connected more with you. They could relate to you. They were starting to like you when we jumped the gun and abandoned you. I am sorry. We are again going with you. I need a win Old, otherwise M will fire me just the way he fired the CMO today. Welcome back. Creating the new logo was a bad idea."

I could not believe David's last words. Such a bastard! He has no backbone, no conviction to protect his own creation. He can't abandon me. He just can't. I could hear that bitch Old's laughter. Loud and clear.

You son of a bitch, you can't abandon me, I am the future. That M has gone stark mad. Tell him that.

I again heard David say, "Welcome back."

If you abandon me, I will kill you David, you will not live to give that bitch a fresh lease of life. You will not live to see that day.

I was lost in my thoughts seething in anger and despair. It was a betrayal I never imagined. From my creator. How could he?

My thoughts were crashed with a loud thud and a blood-cuddling scream. David's.

On the floor was David, covered in his own blood, his head crushed. He was still. Motionless. He was gone.

Beside David was a broken Old, covered in David's blood.

Old looked at me and smirked, "He deserved to die. Should have thought twice before he abandoned me for you. You bitch!"

Life of a Fake

*"Would He wear a pinky ring, would He drive a fancy
     car?
Would His wife wear furs and diamonds, would His
     dressin' room have a star?
If He came back tomorrow, well there's somethin' I'd like
     to know
Could ya tell me, Would Jesus wear a Rolex on His
television show."*

—Would Jesus wear a Rolex by Ray Stevens

Even the thought of this magical word 'Rolex' exudes luxe. Rolex represents the epitome of luxury in most minds. If you are wearing a Rolex, you are a class apart, you 'live for greatness', as they would love to tag themselves. Over ages, US Presidents, leaders and Hollywood stars have given a great legacy to this brand. Rolex means class. It has become a symbol of greatness and power.

Rolex has been able to create a high aspiration quotient for the brand. And thus, to bridge the gap between aspiration and affordability, a category called first copies and fakes have created a huge market for themselves. The first copies are expensive replicas and are better than the fakes in terms of reproduction as well as quality. To even a trained eye, it is not easy to quickly tell the difference between the first copy and the original.

A fake is a notch below.

My story, however, is not told online, it is more of the age-old offline purchase.

I am a fake, of my role model, my idol – the yellow gold Rolex Day Date with diamonds. My creator, a watch master, I call him Master W, does not hail from Switzerland, but from Thailand. He is a gifted septuagenarian, with fifty years of experience in watchmaking. He is an expert in replicating Rolex models. He even trains many watchmen, helping them hone their skills in watch replication.

Legend goes that Master W's watches are even better than the originals.

It must be so painful for him when he reproduces 'Swiss Made' perfectly. I know he must be craving to put his own signature to his creation. His pains are similar to talented forgers, who replicate paintings of great artists. So much talent, but all put in wrong use.

Master W tells his pupils, "We are doing a great service to people. Think of yourselves as enablers. You are helping thousands and thousands of people own your version of a 'Rolex' so that they can flaunt it and be happy."

Master W created me in his workshop.

When he was done with me, he had a proud smile of satisfaction on his face. I love that smile.

A month later, I was at a hi-street market store, waiting eagerly for my buyer. The seller had made me shine like real gold. Master W's craftsmanship was so exquisite that even the glass looked like real diamond.

Trust me, had I been in a Rolex boutique in Bangkok and not on this street store, no one could have spotted the difference. I would have been pampered and my owner would have been proud of have me strapped to his wrist.

But here, on the streets, they bargain as if I have no worth. These people wouldn't even get an entry at the boutique, leave out bargaining. Fate. Why wasn't I born an original in Switzerland?

One day, this fine-looking gentleman came to the store. He was an Indian in his late forties. Manian fell in love with me at first sight. He picked me up, and wore me on his wrist. I fitted beautifully. The store kid was trying to act smart and asked him for a premium. But he had a good knowledge of the rates and bought me at the best price the kid would have got, respecting me.

He took me to his hotel. He kept me very carefully, polished me, and kept looking at me from time to time. After Master W, I saw a glimmer of pride in his smile. Made me feel like my God – the original.

A week passed by and I could see his holidays were almost over and he was planning to leave the next day. In the evening, he had come to the market to buy a smoke. He loved to smoke. His stock from India was over so he had to buy some from the market.

As it was his last evening, he decided to take a stroll in the lanes and bylanes, enjoying me and his smoke. We were having a great time. It was also my last night in Bangkok.

It was dark. I think I saw a shadow move. Perhaps too quickly. I may be wrong. It was really very dark.

After a few minutes I saw the shadow again, just for a moment. A fleeting moment. I know I had seen it. I was beginning to get a strange feeling. As if something was not right.

Maybe I was over analyzing the situation.

Suddenly a tall, dark figure emerged out of nowhere in front of Manian. I was right. I did see the shadow and it was following us. I wanted to warn Manian, but it was too late. In a split second, there was a heavy blow from behind on Manian's head. He immediately pressed his palms against the wound. I was covered in Manian's blood. The two men shouted "Money, money!" Manian could not speak. He was in too much pain, trying his best to stop the blood. They took his fancy wallet, his golden chain and his two golden rings.

While one was about to leave, the bastard who hit him from behind pointed at me. "Rolex", he whispered. He hurriedly took me off Manian's wrist. And they ran away. They took his money and cards, got rid of the wallet.

I don't know whether Manian survived. I really pray he did. I liked him a lot. He had valued even a fake like me.

The bloody thieves realized their mistake the next day when they went to sell me off to their dealer. You should have seen their faces when the dealer laughed out loud at them and told them the reality. I enjoyed their disappointment. For the first time I was happy being a fake.

And after a week, I, the fake Rolex, was back again on another street store waiting for Manian.

Note: Historically, luxury counterfeits were often shipped in large cargo containers and passed through numerous middlemen before reaching the final consumers. However, now counterfeit sellers set up online presences on auction or marketplace sites and ship luxury counterfeits directly to consumers. They also use the internet and social media tools to generate web traffic and to divert consumers to rogue e-commerce websites selling their goods which often have the same look and feel as the brand owner's site. Compared to the purchase of a fake Rolex watch on the street, the purchase of a watch online makes it harder for a consumer to tell whether the product is genuine. An online advertisement by these portals for a Rolex could show a photo of a genuine watch, but the purchaser would actually receive a fake one. The counterfeit seller may create pseudo product reviews, blog entries and rogue social media profiles to enhance its legitimacy. Susceptible consumers may fall for this fake content.*(Ref: Decoding Luxe)*

According to a report by Anna Maria Lagerqvist and Hanna Bruck in Valea International, in 2009 Eurobarometer statistics, 22 per cent of EU citizens have unknowingly bought counterfeit goods. As shopping online is considered entirely legitimate, online counterfeit products may attract consumers who would never purchase a Rolex or Louis Vuitton handbag in a dark alley. The internet creates a situation where the marketplaces for counterfeit products and for the genuine article are suddenly the same.

Further, online shops give the buyer a sense of anonymity and impunity. Given the seemingly boundless scope of the internet, luxury brand owners come across anonymous online counterfeit sellers every day.

Death of a Non-fake

Why is my verse so barren of new pride?
So far from variation or quick change?
Why with the time do I not glance aside
To new-found methods, and to compounds strange?
Why write I still all one, ever the same,
And keep invention in a noted weed,
That every word doth almost tell my name,
Showing their birth and where they did proceed?
O, know, sweet love, I always write of you,
And you and love are still my argument;
So all my best is dressing old words new,
Spending again what is already spent.
For as the sun is daily new and old,
So is my love still telling what is told.

—Sonnet 76: *Why Is My Verse So Barren Of New Pride?*
by William Shakespeare

I was made in a hamlet in Venice. Handcrafted by a master craftsman – I am a deer-skin coffee-coloured long wallet. I was shipped to India for their store in its capital Delhi in a luxury mall. The boutique manager very carefully placed me on the glass showcase, giving me a prominent display.

Indians are very price-sensitive. They look for value for money in every purchase. The boutique manager was a smooth-talker and he was very good at making it worth the money for every customer. They left as happy customers and stayed loyal to the brand. There were so many times, that people used to come and experience the luxury leather goods, writing instruments, watches and jewellery. They kept coming back, again and again, experiencing a bit more every time, till they were finally convinced of the purchase.

Karthik was such a customer. He was not rich but had great appreciation for craftsmanship. He used to spend a lot of time at the boutique, appreciating the new and old collections alike. He had a special liking for me. I came to know Karthik was a blogger of luxury products – he wrote stories about craftsmanship as well as about new collections.

The store manager liked him a lot, and had observed his liking for me. He named a special price for Karthik and finally, I belonged to him.

I have heard him speaking at length with the store manager on the rise of fakes and replicas in the market. They were making them so well that more and more people were drawn towards them. Karthik told the boutique manager how fakes of Rolex, Louis Vuitton and Cartier were hampering the sales figures and growth of these companies. Luxury counterfeits is not a new phenomenon, Karthik continued, but with technological advances and sophisticated new ways to reach consumers, the business is increasing rapidly. The size of counterfeit luxury industry in India is currently about five per cent of the overall market size of India's luxury industry, which currently is worth over $14 billion. With a share of about seven per cent, fake luxury products account for over $22 billion of the global luxury industry worth about $320 billion.

I also came to know over eighty per cent of the imitation luxury products being sold in India come from China and most of these consists of handbags, watches, shoes, clothes, hats, sunglasses, perfumes and jewellery.

Karthik had a fascination for Rolex watches. So much so that all his knowledge and arguments against using counterfeits seemed to vanish when it came to Rolex.

"Someday I will be able to own one, if not the original, the next best thing, a replica," he said. The only difference was, this time, I was inside his sling bag. To talk about a fake in such an aspirational tone when he is a proud owner of me was sacrilege. It saddened me deeply, especially coming from a knowledgeable person like him.

He used to take great care of me. He loved my skin. His fingers always used to linger on me. I was 'his precious'.

Carrying a long wallet is mostly a pain. You do not always wear a jacket, so he used to keep me in his sling bag. Only for me, he would carry the sling. Poor Karthik.

For his writing, he used to travel a lot, mostly abroad. We had been together now for over a year. And I dutifully took care of his money and cards. I have travelled to Paris, London and New York.

This time he was travelling to Bangkok to explore the market there for fake luxury goods for his next story.

We were in Bangkok the following week. Karthik went for a walk to the local market of fakes. I hate fakes. Even the sound makes me puke. The moment I entered the fake market, it was nauseating. I couldn't believe my eyes how my rich heritage and that of my fellow brands was insulted here. This is outrageous. How can they do it? Is copying the looks enough? Where will they get our legacy? I wanted to tell Karthik to not spend even a second here, to go back.

Imagine my shock when I saw him actually walking into a store and buying a fake watch, his weakness. What is wrong with him? He took the ugly-looking fake to the hotel and kept studying it for hours. He was looking at the elements by which you can recognize a fake for his story. I felt sad that he was beginning to develop a liking for the fake watch.

Nonetheless, it was finally time to leave for home. It was our last night here and Karthik decided to take a stroll while enjoying his smoke. He was not carrying his sling and I was popping out of his back pocket.

Suddenly, out of the blue, I saw from the back pocket a dark figure rapidly approaching him with an iron rod. I wanted to shout and warn Karthik, but I couldn't. The son of a bitch hit Karthik hard on the head within a blink. He had a partner who approached from the front. Karthik was seething in pain, with blood oozing from his head. They shouted, "Money, money!" They took me, his gold chain and two rings. They were about to leave, but the bastard who hit him spotted the fake Rolex watch, imagine the fake watch. They took it from his wrist and vanished into the darkness.

Poor Karthik Manian, I pray he survives the injury. I know I will never see him again. I liked him a lot. I was in the hands of the dark figure. He had worn the watch. The idiot thought it is was an original. Suits him! They were crossing the bridge. He opened me up and emptied the money and cards. And threw me into the water. The bastard had no idea that I am the original, and the watch is a fake. And within a few seconds, I hit the cold Chao Phraya River, my burial.

And then my journey towards my slow, painful, decaying death started. It is just a matter of time as I wait to meet my end.

Life of a Roadrunner

You got a fast car
I want a ticket to anywhere
Maybe we make a deal
Maybe together we can get somewhere
Anyplace is better
Starting from zero got nothing to lose
Maybe we'll make something
Me, myself I got nothing to prove.

– 'Fast Car' by Tracy Chapman

Sher Singh was a farmer. One fine day, two men in a suit and a shiny foreign extra-long car came to him and handed him four suitcases filled with money. They made him sign a document and ensured they would come every year to deliver a similar amount. All for leasing a chunk of his Gurgaon farmland. The land remained his and he would get the lease amount every year, in cash, for the next ninety-nine years. These suits would build a township on his land. He looked up in the sky and thanked his grandfather. He was a rich man – now Sher Singh Saab.

He still loved to farm, so he used to spend his days in the residual farmland.

He just had one problem in life. How would he spend the money? A friend suggested he buy a car. He loved driving his tractor and it was his best mode of transport. So if he would buy a car, it had to be a big one.

One fine day, Sher Singh went to the newly-opened luxury car showroom in the city along with his two childhood farmer friends on his tractor. The watchman stopped them, and told them this was not for them. The watchman was forced to push them aside as they persisted. One of his friends got angry and slapped the watchman, the other friend held him strongly and shouted to Sher Singh to enter the showroom.

The commotion made the manager come to the door and stop Sher. He shouted in Hindi: "You know who I am? You bastard, which is the most expensive car here? I will buy that now while you lick my feet." On hearing this, the manager, a sound salesman, apologized. He scolded the watchman and asked him to apologize and usher his two friends in. The manager requested them to sit. He said, "We are extremely sorry, sir. We couldn't recognize you. What will you have? Champagne?"

Sher asked one of his friends to get the jute sack from his tractor. The manger guessed what could be in it and asked the watchman to get it instead.

"*Daru pila. Saaley gaddi dikha.*" (Give me the booze and show the damn car).

The manager showed his pride and joy   Me, the yellow Hummer H3. The manager started praising me in Hindi for Sher Singh, "Sir, Hummer H3, this beast has a 3700 cc engine, with maximum power 239 Bhp @ 5800 rpm, maximum Torque 326 Nm @ 4600 rpm, ground clearance 246 mm, kerb weight 2134 kg and fuel tank capacity of 88 litres..."

Sher Singh stopped him, "*Ready kar isko. Abhi leke jaana hai. Jinta daam hai jholey sey nikal ley. Aur apna tip bhi. Jab bhi mujhe dekhega khare hoke salaam mar nuch   e!*" (Get it ready, will take it home now. Take the money from the bag also keep your tip. You bastard, whenever you see me, stand up and salute!)

The friend poured the entire money from the sack on the floor. The manager knew from the start it was a closed deal. He immediately instructed his staff to do the needful while he entertained Sher and his friends with more champagne.

Sher Singh had not driven a car in a long time. The last he drove was his uncle's Ambassador a few years back.

But I could see he was very happy. He immediately named me after him – 'Shera'.

Sher Singh had a huge house. His family was surprised to see me and they immediately did a pooja and put a tilak on me.

I love the attention. And why not?

The next morning, Sher took me out for a spin. Although the village roads were challenging, I was tougher. Both Sher and Shera loved it.

He started talking to me. Praising me for being so tough. He loved his tractor and kept comparing me with it. I didn't mind as he did it in a loving way.

Sher, the Jat with a *gamchha* around his head, was my owner. This was a new experience.

Sher was not sure what to do with the huge space that I had. His two idiot friends suggested to carry sugarcane and other farm produce in me to the market. Can you even image those scoundrels' audacity?

To my utter horror, Sher agreed. From the next day, I had become the carrier of farm produce to the market. I was reduced to an ugly tempo or a tractor. I really prayed no one could see me, especially my fellow Hummers. I preferred to do my chores with blinders, like city horses. As you know, although initially there were trucks made under my brand by American Motors Company, later when General Motors took over, they made me a class apart, an aspiration – Humvee. I serve the Army as well as the Richie Rich alike.

Sher always used to enjoy the attention of the women in the village when he drove his Shera.

Sher and his two friends took me for a ride to booze and watch 'hot babes'. Yes, these two words were a part of their limited English vocabulary. They wanted to know whether these girls and, if luck favoured, firangs, were impressed with Shera. It may be their day to get lucky, they said.

One of them said, *"Yaar koi film jaisi nicker pehenewali hot firangi gori ko Shera ki godi mein chadha pata toh mazaa aa jaata*" (If we could give a skimpily clad hot foreign girl, just like in the English films, a ride, it would be awesome). I knew their desperation to sleep with 'hot firangs'. They watch these films, mostly adult ones in their phones, inside me. I have seen their lust while watching these films. But that's okay, men will be men.

The entire day, they had made cat calls to girls in short skirts or long, hot pants or jeans or trousers, crop tops or even sarees. Basically they teased each and every girl they could.

In the late evening, they drove me to a locality I was not very familiar with. I could sense these women were sex workers. It was obvious from their response to the teasing of these three. They stopped outside an old house and the three of them went in. I waited. They came back after two hours, sloshed. There was a skinny person who came out to see them off. Sher's friend said in Hindi, "You bastard, you had promised us gori firangs."

The guy said, "Sir, but weren't the girls *gori chitti* (fair)? Weren't they good? They are models, sir. Absolutely fitting your class. The Russian, who was supposed to come, ditched at the last moment. I will call you when I can arrange for them."

I could see the four girls on the balcony. They were very pretty, admiring me.

We left. We were on our way to the village.

It was very late in the night. All three were sloshed, already down four, or more, and on another bottle of scotch, neat. Sher was driving me. I was a little scared because it was late in the night and all of them were drunk. And you know I am a beast. Thankfully, the roads were very well lit.

Suddenly, Sher saw a girl in a spaghetti top riding a Scooty. The roads were completely empty. Sher honked. She was not wearing a helmet, and they could see her face when she turned upon hearing the horn. She was a foreigner. Suddenly, Sher took me beside her bike and shouted, "Madam, English?" His friends joined the teasing. The girl gave them a stern look and showed them her middle finger. She sped ahead to avoid them. What are these idiots doing? Why are they teasing the girl? Have they gone completely insane?

Sher and his friends started shouting and calling her 'bitch'. One of the friends told him, "*Utha ley. Aaj hum film jaisa maza lenge.*" (Pick her up. We will have fun like these guys in the movies.)

Sher gulped some more scotch from the bottle. He told me, "*Chal Shera, pakad lo*" (Catch her, Shera).

Had he gone mad? He started chasing the girl. The girl increased the speed further, but I am a beast. A Scooty will not stand any chance in front of me. Sher planned to cross her and take a sharp turn and jam the brakes in front of her bike, forcing her to stop. This is not an easy task when I am at top speed, especially when you are not a good driver and you are sloshed. All three of them were shouting and calling her a bitch, threatening to rape her. Sher was just turning me and suddenly the girl tried to speed past me. Instead of the brakes, Sher jammed the accelerator. Within a blink, I accidentally hit her scooter and the girl was air-borne for a few seconds before she came crashing on the road, a few feet away, in front of me. The Scooty was smashed. And so was the girl. I could see her move a little. She was covered in blood and so was my headlamp. Then she went still.

Shera had immediately jammed the brakes. But it was too late. Everything was over. The three of them didn't even realize what had just happened.

When they got out of their stupor, the friend from behind shouted "*Bhaag Sher bhag!*" (Run). Sher Singh immediately hit the accelerator and rushed away, leaving the girl to die.

I killed an innocent girl that night.

Note: If you check Wikipedia, you will know about my rich heritage. The original Hummers were designed by AM General Corporation. The Humvee replaced the military Jeeps that were produced by American Motors Corporation until 1982. In 1979, the United States Army was seeking contractors for a new 'High Mobility Multi-Purpose Wheeled Vehicle' which could follow the tracks and ruts of full size army trucks (HMMWV). At that time, General Dynamics, Teledyne, and Chrysler Defense had HMMWV designs under development. Among the four competitors for the contract, AM General designed an entirely new vehicle to meet the Army's requirements. In less than one year, it was the first to deliver a prototype vehicle. Initial production versions were delivered to the Army's proving grounds in April 1982. After testing was completed, AM General was awarded the contract to supply its HMMWV to the United States armed forces. The first models were built in a variety of military-based equipment and versions. The first contract was in 1983, worth US$1.2 billion to produce 55,000 'Humvees' by 1985. The first production vehicle was assembled by AM General on January 2, 1985. AM General had planned to sell a civilian version of the Humvee as far back as the late 1980s. The civilian model began in part because of the persistence of Arnold Schwarzenegger, who saw an Army convoy while filming a movie.

Death of a Golden Nib

Death, be not proud, though some have called thee
Mighty and dreadful, for thou are not so;
For those whom thou think'st thou dost overthrow
Die not, poor Death, nor yet canst thou kill me.
From rest and sleep, which but thy pictures be,
Much pleasure; then from thee much more must flow,
And soonest our best men with thee do go,
Rest of their bones, and soul's delivery.
Thou'art slave to fate, chance, kings, and desperate men,
And dost with poison, war, and sickness dwell,
And poppy'or charms can make us sleep as well
And better than thy stroke; why swell'st thou then?
One short sleep past, we wake eternally,
And death shall be no more; Death, thou shalt die."

—'Death, Be Not Proud' by John Donne

I was inside him, dangling from his neck. Blood oozing from the punctured vein. My nib broke inside him, the broken part still clinging tightly to his skin.

Charles removed me from his neck and punctured it again. And again, and again. Stephen struggled to contain his blood, but in vain.

He fell on the floor. There was blood all over. I kept cutting Stephen's arteries and veins till he went still.

Charles removed me from the neck. My nib was broken, my breather hole slit, tipping material, shoulder, almost till the imprint was attached to his skin. He cleaned the blood on my feed, body and base with his handkerchief. He removed the broken nib from the neck. He put on the lid and I was in his pocket. He slid the broken nib carefully inside his pocket.

Stephen was lying on the floor. Lifeless.

And when I left the room, I was no longer a luxury writing instrument. I had become a murder weapon.

I have blood on me. The blood of my owner.

The irony is that Stephen had plans to gift me to Charles on his upcoming birthday so that he could start appreciating a fine writing instrument.

Charles picked up the blood-stained file from the floor that Stephen gave his life to protect and left the house. I know what is inside the file; I had written it.

I am a Writer's Edition – William Shakespeare MB writing instrument. On my golden nib is etched the writer's signature.

My owner Stephen and I were together for ten long years. Always together. And now he is no more. And I belong to a murderer – Charles. My broken nib misses me, misses Stephen.

On his way home, Charles carefully disposed of the blood-stained nib and his handkerchief in the Arno river.

I was still there in his pocket.

Reaching his home, Charles headed straight for the study.

He poured himself his favourite Macallan Lalique 50 Year Old. He had gifted the same brand to Stephen on his last birthday.

He was his closest friend, his colleague. Stephen used to love him. How could he kill him? How could he make me, Stephen's favourite writing instrument, a murder weapon? I will never be able to forgive myself. Never. I wished Charles had thrown me into the river as well.

Anyway, as I am a Writer's Edition, MB has broken my cast long back, so he will not be able to replace my nib. I will never be able to write. Why does he want to keep me? What's the use? Charles knew how much Stephen loved me. Charles was not into writing instruments any which way; he only used cheap ball point pens.

And Stephen loved him so much that he had decided to part with me for him.

Charles carefully placed me and the file on his writing desk.

He sat and started sipping his poison, his eyes were glued on me and the file. Kept on tapping the chair's armrest. I sensed a little anxiety in his body language, as if he was waiting for something.

What was I missing?

I am sure Charles murdered Stephen because he wanted to steal the content of the file – the secret biological formula that Stephen had discovered and the notes on the possibilities of a maximum impact. All that meant for the well-being of mankind. He had written all that using me and placed it inside the file. Tomorrow, he was supposed to share it with the owner of the pharma company Mr T. Both Charles and Stephen are chief scientists in Mr T's company. Stephen was a genius and he would have saved lives of millions using this formula. Now I am sure this bastard will sell it to terrorists and kill millions.

The doorbell rang. Charles rushed to open it. I could hear Charles shout, "Where is my son?"

"Dr Charles, did you manage to get the formula?"

He walked in with two suited men. The traitor handed the file to the younger one. He opened it and started scrutinizing the papers, while the older person patiently sipped the drink with a smile on his face.

"He is safe with his mother. You may call her and confirm," he said with his smile intact.

Charles immediately called his ex-wife and spoke to Jim. Tears rolled down his eyes.

Charles screamed at the man and demanded an answer, "Today, I murdered my friend. I am so sorry, Stephen. Why did you make me do it?"

The two men didn't respond. When the younger one was finished with the file and was satisfied, he handed it over to the senior. He took the file, placed it carefully inside the bag and spoke to Charles, "Did you make a copy of it, Dr Charles?" He frantically shook his head and said no. "Good. Otherwise, I would have had to kill you." He smiled.

He pulled out his cell phone and made a quick call, "Madame Secretary, we have averted the crisis. We have the formula. Dr C has 'convinced' Dr S."

He carefully listened to the instructions at the other end of the call and then closed the call.

He spoke again, "I will request you to calm down and listen to us. We had information that Dr Stephen was developing a formula for a deadly biological weapon for your boss Mr T, and was planning to sell it to the highest bidder in the black market. Rumour has it the price could have run into a few hundred millions. Dr Stephen would have retired a rich man bagging millions himself. Mr T and Dr Stephen both knew you would not take part in such a heinous crime that will be used by terrorists to kill millions of innocent civilians, so they had kept you in the dark.

Charles knew they were up to something, from the sudden increase in interactions between Stephen and T. For the past one year, Stephen had been mum on his research, dodging every query of Charles. But a biological weapon for mass murder? T could do anything, but Stephen? He kept silent.

"We could not reveal to you our identity earlier because it was an issue of national security. So we knew you would not believe us if we told you that your friend was a traitor. Honestly, we were also not certain that you were not part of the plan. We could not take chances. We had to keep your son in our custody. We never intended to harm him.

They flashed their ID cards.

Sorry, what? I couldn't believe my ears.

He continued: "We had no proof, so we could not arrest Dr Stephen or Mr T, or stop them. But we were certain that even if we foiled this attempt, Dr Stephen and T might come up with something else, even more deadlier. We had to eliminate the source. We were forced to use you. We know you studied medicine for two years and were good in anatomy before you decided to pursue bio-technology because you wanted to provide cheaper medicines to the masses. We knew, only you could have executed it without a conventional weapon, without leaving a trail."

Charles shouted, "I have committed a heinous crime. Killed

my own friend and you are now telling me that he was a traitor?"

The calm voice took out a recorder and played it. It was my owner's voice, he was speaking to T. They had intercepted a phone conversation. "We have been tapping their conversations and this one is just two days old."

It was Stephen's voice. Stephen was telling T that he had made the deadliest biological weapon mankind has ever seen, so he wanted no less than twenty per cent and not five per cent, as decided earlier. He had also made the perfect plan for maximum impact. Stephen was proudly selling his prowess of enabling terrorists to kill millions of innocent civilians. Stephen told T that Charles is asking a lot of questions about his research. To this, T said, "Stephen, you need to eliminate all loose ends if you want your twenty per cent. And Stephen, you need to make it quick."

I couldn't believe my ears, neither could Charles.

How could Stephen do it? How could he? Greed had consumed him.

I realized Stephen had already used me to pen down the killer formula and the detailed plan for maximum impact.

Charles was silent.

The two men stood up to leave.

The senior person said calmly, "Charles, your contribution towards the nation is priceless. The country and the Agency are indebted to you."

Charles remained seated while they walked away.

He finished his drink and stood up. He was still crying. He came towards me, held me up, opened my lid and focused on my broken nib.

He said, "Why did you do it, Stephen? But still, I am so sorry. I will always keep your favourite pen close to me as your memory."

Charles is a good man.

I could never forgive a traitor. I am glad millions of lives were saved.

Life of the Golden Scissors

A People and their King
Through ancient sin grown strong,
Because they feared no reckoning
Would set no bound to wrong;
But now their hour is past,
And we who bore it find
Evil Incarnate held at last
To answer to mankind.
For agony and spoil
Of nations beat to dust,
For poisoned air and tortured soil
And cold, commanded lust,
And every secret woe
The shuddering waters saw—
Willed and fulfilled by high and low—
Let them relearn the Law:

— 'Justice' by Rudyard Kipling

I have given birth only to the first-born heirs to the throne. I have liberated them, made them independent human beings by severing their umbilical cords for generations!

I love the taste of blood. I love the taste of royalty. Without me, they will cease to exist.

I am the sharpest of them all. I give life, but I can also be the deadliest weapon. I can cut the vein and watch the blood ooze from the wrist till death comes to take you away. The blood on my golden body looks majestic.

I was crafted by a master goldsmith at a special request from the Maharaja himself. The Maharaja wanted a pair of golden scissors, beautifully crafted and designed. One that would be an integral part of royalty. The Maharaja after the premature death of his second son was desperate for a male heir. He was advised by the Raj Purohit that during birth of royalty for the bloodline to survive, the umbilical cord needs to be only severed by a golden pair of scissors after a special puja. It was impossible for a golden pair of scissors to have the sharpness to severe such ties so the Maharaja had to take help from my Creator, Master Goldsmith. Only he knew the magic to make me as sharp as a sword!

When I severed the first umbilical cord of the heir to the throne, it was a matter of great honour. The child survived and after thirty years, became the Maharaja. I have been with the family for two centuries now. I was the knight in shining armour who kept death at bay for the royalty. Until that dreaded night.

Maharaja Mahadev Singh was desperately awaiting the sound of the first cry of his first born. He was a fierce warrior. Only twenty-two, but had been able to establish his empire of terror far and wide. A ruthless king, he did not believe in humanity and love. His only wish was an heir, a son.

Suddenly, he heard the first cry.

It was a centuries-old ritual that the Maharaja himself would use me to sever the cord.

The attendant called him to perform the ritual. She said, "Congratulations, mighty Maharaj, the Queen has given birth to a beautiful princess."

The words hit him like an arrow. In a blink, he took his sword and beheaded the attendant.

He rushed in, the queen was still not completely conscious.

The next sixty seconds witnessed the darkest event in the history of the kingdom.

The blood-cuddling scream of the attendant had scared away the rest. The Queen was all alone, unconscious, with the baby.

He saw the baby. He threw away the sword. He took me, and instead of cutting the cord, he pushed me into the heart of the queen. And then left her to die. The queen didn't even have the power to take me out. She died in her slumber. All alone, crying, was the baby girl who remained attached to the dying queen.

I would make him pay the price!

Death of a Slumber

A slumber did my spirit seal;
I had no human fears:
She seemed a thing that could not feel
The touch of earthly years.

No motion has she now, no force;
She neither hears nor sees;
Rolled round in earth's diurnal course,
With rocks, and stones, and trees.

—William Wordsworth

Slumber is a luxury! Ask any billionaire, Maharaja, President or Prime Minister. They will tell you that I am their ultimate luxury, something that money can't buy, ever.

There are times when these very important men, in the fear of chronic sleep deprivation, take help of medicines that relax their senses and help them get good sleep. There are also times, when I help people get into a deeper slumber so that their transition from life to death becomes painless.

Maharaja Mahadev Singh was a fierce warrior, but he had committed a brutality which was not human. He had murdered his queen, immediately after child-birth, and had left his first-born to die. I helped the queen make the transition in the most painless way possible, in spite of the golden scissors jutting out from her heart. I, the slumber, held her close to myself, till she passed on. I also helped the baby go to sleep. I knew she would not survive for long, without milk, once the mother was dead. I sang her a lullaby for her to go to sleep. I couldn't see her in so much pain.

While the Maharaja was busy expanding his reign of terror, his brother Bhudev Singh was busy searching for an opportunity to kill his brother and ascend the throne. But he was a coward.

He always had an eye for the golden pair of scissors as it was only meant for the future Maharaja. He was 'not worthy' of it during his birth, unlike his brother's. So he will use it for killing his brother to tell him that Bhudev also is worthy of the coveted pair of scissors.

After that dreadful dark night of the murder of the queen and her child, I and the golden scissors had promised to avenge this crime. So from that night onwards, we targeted Bhudev because of his greed for the throne. Every night after that dark night during his slumber, I started slowly infecting Bhudev Singh with a thought – he is born to be a King! And the only way he can become a King is by killing his brother.

"Kill him and fulfil your dream. Become the King!"

Finally, after thirty nights, he came up with the perfect plan and the courage to commit the murder of his brother.

He increased the morphine dosage of his brother conspiring with the family doctor or Raj Vaidya. When he knew the action of the morphine was at its peak, he drove the golden scissors straight into his brother's heart. Mahadev was very strong, much stronger than Bhudev. In one blow, he was able to throw his brother on the ground. But just as he was trying to remove from his chest my new friend of justice, the golden scissors, I held him back. I overpowered him and kept him still. I completely overpowered him. Then I waited for death to take him away.

Yes, I did feel his fading resistance. I did feel how death had started to work on him and how life was ready to take a flight.

Slowly, I overpowered him completely. He was calm, awaiting his transition.

The golden scissors didn't have to fight anymore.

No motion has he now, no force!

Tailpiece: Life of a Python

Death kisses me, Sucking the oxygen from my lungs,
A kiss so deadly, It can only be felt once,
A kiss of death so seductive, You'll never come back,
You get a taste of what can be, you get a taste of what you
*   lack,*
Death lays you upon a bed of crimson love,
You feel the moisture, seeping through your clothes,
You look down as your eyes fill with delight,
You see your wrists dripping, Growing this bed of lustful
fright,
You let out a gentle moan, for these pleasure you've never
*   known,*
Who knew death would feel so right.
Lines blur. my vision fades,
Darkness; faded into this one, eternal, night.
Let death encase me with its final shroud of shadows.
So enthralled you take a final breath,
The lips of death beckon you, You have no choice..
You humbly accept."

—'A Kiss of Death' by Crimson Love

It was love at first sight for MB. He had been looking for this for the past four years. And finally, it was there, showcased at the window of a store in Venice. The first feeling was experiential, the feeling of joy when you discover something that you have been searching for long. But after a few moments, the mind sets in – it may be a fake or may be very expensive if it is genuine. Harrowed by the questions of the mind, which had already taken his enthusiasm down a few notches, he decides to enter the store and find out.

The store manager was happy to show it to him. "You can even feel the scales," she told him. MB touched it for the first time. A chill ran down his spine. This was the luxe, the dazzle. It was as if he was touching a real python. The wallet was perfect and there was no doubt that it was real python skin. The genuine exotic leather plus the luxury brand premium made the price seem a little on the steeper side, but MB knew the price was right. He felt the skin and scales again and closed the deal immediately.

Finally, after such a long search, he owned the perfect python-skin long wallet of his favourite luxe brand. He felt on top of the world.

He went home with his precious possession. Every time he touched the skin, it felt so real. Even a little cold. It was as if the wallet was his pet python. He kept is safely in the drawer; he feared if he used it every day the scales will wear off and his pet python will shed its skin. So every day he would open the drawer, feel the skin and put it back. Just like a pet in a cage.

It was a month later when he held the wallet in his hands, that he was shocked to see that the scales were coming off. The skin has gone dull! He immediately put it back in the dark drawer. He was scared that even after so much care he had not been able to keep the scales intact. He felt very sad. As if all the hard work had gone down the drain.

He was so scared that he waited a whole week before he summoned the courage to open the drawer slowly and put his hands inside to pull out the wallet. His fingers touched something cold. He immediately withdrew his hands. Curiosity took the better of him and he brought the torchlight and flashed it inside. He couldn't believe his eyes.

Besides the wallet was a separate python skin! Much bigger than the size of the wallet.

He couldn't help it, so he touched the skin again. It was cold, the scales were real. It was the shed skin of a python.

But how was it possible? He could see there was a shine on the skin of his wallet.

Something strange happened in the next moment. He felt very happy and became distanced from reality. It was a strange lure that forced him to forget the fear, touch his wallet and kiss it. Made his lips feel the fresh skin.

He immediately brought the wallet out. The skin was shining bright, luring and mesmerizing him. It was the magic that made him stop by the store window and possess it. He gave it a kiss, and his lips felt the cold, fresh skin of the python.

Everything went dark for MB. Suddenly, there was no air to breathe. But somehow he had a smile on his face. He never struggled. Slowly he could feel he was engulfed by the python. Slowly he went numb, slowly he felt the cold. Slowly he felt the stillness of death.

Epilogue

An ode to Darkness

I had a dream, which was not all a dream.
The bright sun was extinguish'd, and the stars
Did wander darkling in the eternal space,
Rayless, and pathless, and the icy earth
Swung blind and blackening in the moonless air;
Morn came and went—and came, and brought no day,
And men forgot their passions in the dread
Of this their desolation; and all hearts
Were chill'd into a selfish prayer for light:
And they did live by watchfires—and the thrones,
The palaces of crowned kings- -the huts,
The habitations of all things which dwell,
Were burnt for beacons; cities were consum'd,
And men were gather'd round their blazing homes
To look once more into each other's face;

—'Darkness' by Lord Byron

It was during a trip through the dark catacombs of St Stephen's Cathedral in Vienna that a thought dawned on me. The Stephen's Cathedral houses the tombs of Prince Eugene of Savoy (PES), commander of the Imperial forces during the War of the Spanish Succession in the Chapel of The Cross (northwest corner of the cathedral) and of Frederick III, Holy Roman Emperor (Fr3), under whose reign the Diocese of Vienna was canonically erected on 18 January 1469, in the Apostles' Choir (southeast corner of the cathedral). The basement of the cathedral also houses the crypts of Bishops, Provosts and Ducal. The most recent interment in the Bishop's crypt completed in 1952 under the south choir was that of ninety-eight-year-old Cardinal Franz König in 2004. Provosts of the cathedral are buried in another chamber.

When you see the seemingly-innocent urns, little would you know what they contain. The Ducal Crypt located under the chancel holds seventy-eight bronze containers with the bodies, hearts, or viscera of seventy-two members of the Habsburg dynasty. Before his death in 1365, Duke Rudolf IV ordered the crypt built for his remains in the new cathedral he commissioned. By 1754, the small rectangular chamber was overcrowded with twelve sarcophagi and thirty-nine urns, so the area was expanded with an oval chamber added to the east end of the rectangular one. In 1956, the two chambers were renovated and their contents rearranged. The sarcophagi of Duke Rudolf IV and his wife were placed upon a pedestal and the sixty-two urns containing organs were moved from the two rows of shelves around the new chamber to cabinets in the original one.

This was history, courtesy Wikipedia, but here is the interesting bit – when the charnel house and eight cemeteries abutting the cathedral's side and back walls closed due to an outbreak of bubonic plague in 1735, the bones within them were moved to the catacombs below the church. Burials directly in the catacombs occurred until 1783, when a new law forbade most burials within the city.

It is very cold inside the catacombs. You will get an eerie feeling, a feeling of some presence. Suddenly my curiosity made me peep through a window into a dimly-lit room. My blood cuddled and a chill ran through my spines. Yes I am using clichés, as sometimes they best describe your feelings. It was a room of death. Human bones and skulls were stacked neatly in the room. And then this was only one of the rooms – the rooms of death. The remains of over 11,000 persons are in the catacombs – just their bones and skulls.

After gathering my nerves, I looked into the next room and then the next – no glass barriers, only a window. After a few windows and innovative patterns with which human bones and skulls can be stacked, I felt nauseated.

It was at that moment that this thought dawned on me – have I given the readers of *Dark Luxe* a similar experience?

Are my stories like these rooms of death?

Maybe, maybe not. But that is for my readers to let me know.

Like the walls of the catacomb, luxury remains a silent witness to the darkness of human deeds.

Let me know your feelings: mahul.brahma@gmail.com
Twitter: @mahulbrahma